Add It

Dip It

Fix It

Add It

Dip

HOUGHTON MIFFLIN COMPANY   BOSTON

It

Fix It

A BOOK OF VERBS

by R. M. Schneider

For Daniel and Rebecca, my children, my friends

Manufactured in the United States of America

Book design by David Saylor
The text of this book is set in 119 point ITC Weidemann Black.
The illustrations are cut-paper collages, reproduced in full color.

BVG   10   9   8   7   6   5   4   3   2

Library of Congress Cataloging-in-Publication Data
Schneider, R. M. (Richard Marlowe)
Add It, Dip It, Fix It / by R. M. Schneider
p.   cm.   ISBN 0-395-72771-5
1. English language—Verb—Juvenile literature.   I. Title.
PE1271.S25   1995   428.2—dc20   94-40743
CIP   AC

We...

add

i+t=it

box

climb

dip

eat

fix

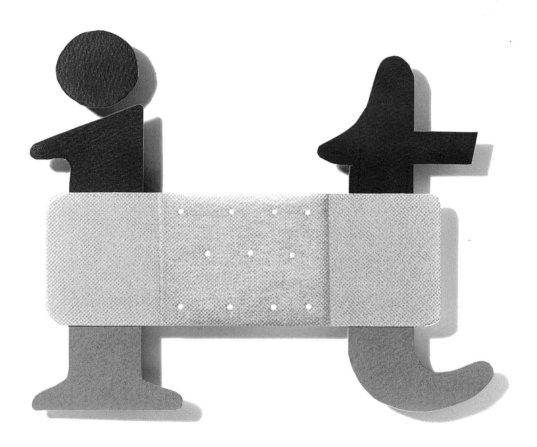

grab

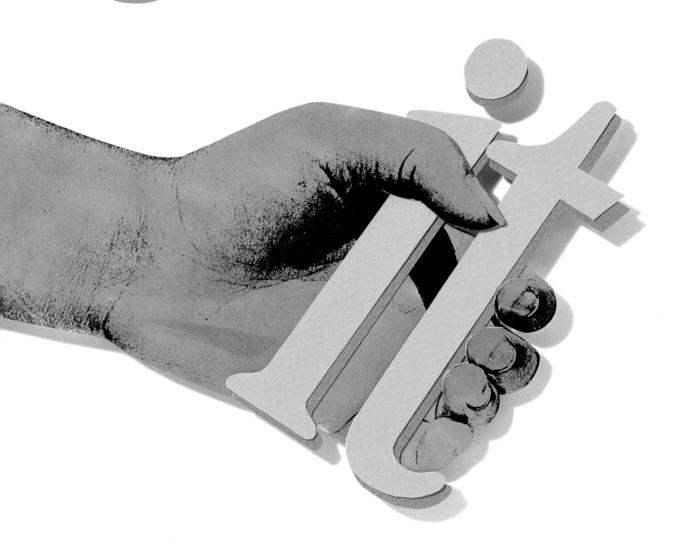

hatch

it

iron

join

kick

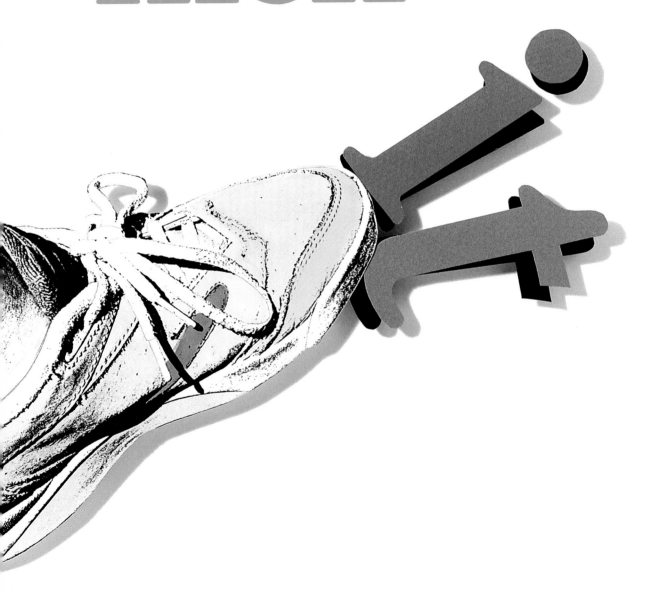

lift

move

nail

open

paint

quilt

rip it

sew

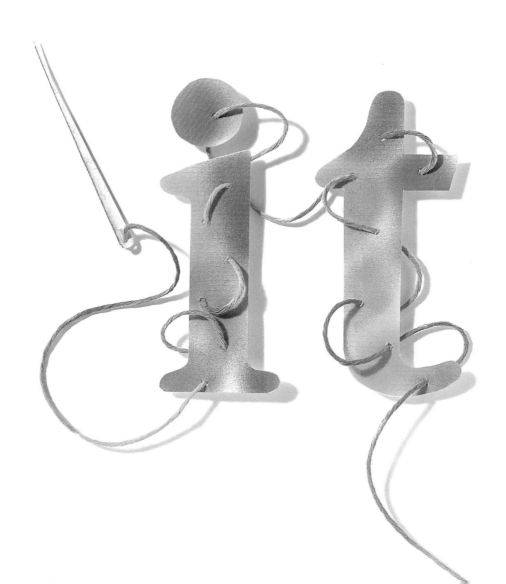

tie

unlock

vacuum

water

x-ray

zip

and that is